Mia
the Bridesmaid
Fairy

by Daisy Meadows

ORCHARD BOOKS

www.rainbowmagic.co.uk

Jack Frost's
Ice Castle

Fields

Kenbury Village

Esther's
House

Church

Moorland

Wishing Well

Rain clouds brew and ice winds blow,
Seek out weddings high and low.
Blemish all the snow-white dresses,
Drizzle on their shining tresses.

Goblins, heed my cold command,
And travel to the human land.
These fairy charms I bid you hide,
To spoil the dreams of every bride!

The Silver Sixpence

Contents

Wedding Plans

"Isn't it exciting that we're going to be Esther's bridesmaids?" said Rachel Walker happily.

"Yes, I can hardly wait for next Saturday!" replied Kirsty Tate, smiling at her best friend. "And it'll be twice as much fun with you here!"

The girls were in Kenbury, the pretty little village where Esther, Kirsty's cousin, had grown up. The sun was shining brightly and there wasn't a cloud in the sky. It was perfect wedding weather.

Esther, Mrs Tate and Aunt Isabel, Esther's mum, were in the wedding dress shop, but the girls had popped out to look at the lovely church where Esther was going to get married.

"Oh Kirsty, look!" cried Rachel. "There must be a wedding today!"

People were arriving in their best clothes, carrying cameras and little boxes of confetti.

"And there's the vicar!" Kirsty added in excitement.

A lady in a long cassock was standing at the church gate.

"Hello girls," she said, smiling. "Are you here for the wedding?"

"Not today," said Kirsty, smiling back at her. "My cousin Esther is getting married here next Saturday, and we're her bridesmaids."

"We've just been looking at the wedding dress," added Rachel.

She pointed at a little shop across the road. Above the window hung an old-fashioned sign:

Rachel and Kirsty caught each other's eyes and grinned. They knew all about magic, because they shared an amazing secret. They were good friends with the Rainbow Magic fairies, and they often helped them to defeat mean Jack Frost and his naughty goblin servants.

A cream car drew up outside the church, and a smart chauffeur jumped out and opened the back door. Inside, the girls could see a woman wearing a frothy white dress.

"It's the bride!" Rachel exclaimed. "Isn't she lovely!"

"See you next week then, girls," smiled the vicar. "I've got a wedding to perform!"

Rachel and Kirsty said goodbye and walked back to the wedding shop.

"I love the dress in the window!" said Kirsty.

"Me too," Rachel agreed.

Under an archway of roses, an exquisite wedding dress was surrounded by sprays of real flowers.

"Bella's *such* an amazing dressmaker!" Kirsty said, with a happy sigh.

Just then, Aunt Isabel popped her head out of the shop door.

"Girls, come back inside," she said with a beaming smile. "Bella is ready for you to try on your dresses."

Rachel and Kirsty hurried to the room at the back of the shop. Bella held up two exquisite dresses and the girls' eyes widened.

"Oh, they're beautiful!" Rachel whispered.

They quickly got changed, giggling in anticipation. Then they stood in front of the long mirror.

"Oh girls, you look lovely!" cried Aunt Isabel.

"Just like princesses!" Esther added.

The dresses were pale blue, and they shimmered and sparkled with hundreds of tiny silver beads. Soft frills made the gowns swirl around the girls' legs, and the sleeves were made from fine blue silk, which fluttered when the girls moved their arms.

"They're just like fairy wings!"
whispered Kirsty to Rachel.

Bella checked that the dresses fitted,
and made some small alterations.

"Thank you, girls," she said eventually.
"You can get changed now."

"Our dresses are just gorgeous," sighed
Rachel, smiling at Bella. "We love the
one in the window too. Is it waiting to
be collected?"

"No," said Bella. "It's a copy of one of
my favourites, which I made a long time
ago. I just couldn't bear to part with it,
so I made another!"

"Goodness, you must have made
hundreds of dresses," said Aunt Isabel.
"And I expect you know everything
there is to know about weddings!"

"I've learnt an awful lot," agreed Bella.

"I particularly love all the old traditions, and bridesmaids are one of the oldest traditions of all! It's their job to help

everything to go smoothly for the bride."

The two girls exchanged happy looks.

"What other wedding traditions are there?" Rachel asked.

"Do you know what a bride should carry up the aisle to bring her luck?" asked Bella. "'Something old, something new, something borrowed, something blue, and a sixpence in her shoe'."

"There's nothing wrong with a little extra luck," laughed Esther, who had been trying on tiaras in front of the mirror. "Girls, will you be in charge of finding me four 'somethings' and a sixpence?"

"We'd love to!" Rachel said, eagerly. "Oh look, Rachel!" Kirsty exclaimed, "Let's start by looking over there!"

At the front of the shop, in an alcove alongside the window, was a low table filled with wedding accessories.

The girls dashed over to it, while Mrs Tate, Esther and Aunt Isabel stayed at the back of the shop.

"Look at these delicate bride and groom figures," said Kirsty. "They must be to put on the top of wedding cakes!"

"And here's a little bridesmaid figure!" cried Rachel in delight. "Oh Kirsty, I can hardly wait to be a bridesmaid!"

"Me neither," Kirsty agreed eagerly. "How about if Esther borrows the pretty dragonfly brooch your mum's wearing for the 'something old'?" Rachel suggested.

"That's perfect!" agreed Kirsty. "It's been in the family for years so it's definitely old enough! Now we just have to think of 'something new, something borrowed and something blue'."

"And the 'sixpence for her shoe'," Rachel reminded her. "Oh Kirsty, look!"

She gave her best friend a nudge that made her squeak in surprise. The bridesmaid figure on the table had started to glow!

A Visitor From Fairyland

With a tinkling sound, glittering fairy dust floated down, and shining silver confetti appeared where it landed. In place of the bridesmaid figure stood a tiny fairy, smiling up at the girls. Her dark pink dress flowed over a full net skirt, accessorised with a pale pink bow, and a red rose glowed in her golden hair.

"Hello, girls!" she said in a voice like tiny bells. "I'm Mia the Bridesmaid Fairy!"

"Hi Mia!" the girls replied excitedly, moving further into the alcove so they couldn't be seen by the others.

"Is anything wrong in Fairyland?" Rachel asked anxiously.

The fairies often needed the girls' help when Jack Frost was making mischief.

Mia gave them a warm smile. "Everything's fine. King Oberon and Queen Titania just asked me to sprinkle some extra good-luck fairy dust on your dresses so all the preparations for the wedding go well," she explained. "It's my job to make sure bridesmaids are happy

and that they make the wedding
special!"

Before Kirsty and Rachel could reply
the church bells began to peal. Through
the window they saw the wedding party,
posing for a photograph.

Suddenly, a dark cloud crossed the sun and a gust of wind blew the bride's bouquet out of her hands! It tumbled towards a muddy puddle, and the bridesmaids ran after it.

"The bouquet will be ruined!" Kirsty gasped.

"And the bridesmaids will get mud on their pretty dresses!" Rachel exclaimed.

Mia sent a jet of sparkling magic from her wand. She conjured up a soft breeze that pushed the bouquet away from the puddle and caused it to land safely on the grass. Rachel and Kirsty smiled in relief, but Mia shook her head with a worried expression.

"That's funny," she
said, frowning. "A tiny
bit of magic like that
shouldn't tire me out,
but I feel weaker.
I wonder if anything
is wrong with the
wedding charms – the

three items that give me my
magic powers."

"You do look a little pale," Kirsty
noticed.

"Girls, will you come to Fairyland with
me?" asked Mia. "I must find out what the
problem is before I do any more magic."

"Of course we will!" said Rachel
at once.

Kirsty hurried through to the back of
the shop.

"Mum, is it all right if we go now?"
she asked.

"OK," said Mrs Tate. "We'll see you
back at Aunt Isabel's house in half
an hour!"

Quickly, Kirsty and Rachel ran out of
the shop and down a cobbled alley, with
Mia hiding in Rachel's pocket. When
they were out of sight of the main street,
Mia waved her wand.

Immediately, a glittering stream of
fairy dust burst from the wand's tip.

It swirled around the girls and they felt themselves shrinking to fairy size. Beautiful wings appeared on their backs.

"We're fairies again!" Rachel cried in delight, fluttering in the air.

Mia waved her wand once more and glittering sparks spun around them like a whirlwind, whisking them away in a flurry of fairy dust.

A few moments later, the magical
sparkles faded away and the girls were
flying over Fairyland. Below, they could
see the red-and-white toadstool houses
and the Fairyland Palace.

"Let's go straight to the Wedding
Workshop, to see if there are any clues as
to why I feel weak," Mia said. "It's inside
the palace, so we can visit the king and
queen after that."

"What happens in the Wedding
Workshop?" asked Rachel.

"My fairy helpers make magical flower
garlands and enchanted confetti, and all
sorts of other things that help human
weddings go smoothly," Mia explained.
"It's also where we keep the wedding
charms. As long as they're in the
workshop, my magic remains powerful."

She led them into the palace and
fluttered down in front of two white
doors. "This is the best place to find out
what's wrong with my magic, because—
oh no!"

Mia had pushed the doors open as she
was speaking. The girls saw long tables
scattered with ribbons, strings of pearls
and silks and satins in all colours of the
rainbow. However, there was not a fairy
to be seen. The workshop was deserted!

Goblin
Mischief

"I don't understand!" cried Mia, looking around in shock. "The workshop never closes!"

"Let's go and see the king and queen," Kirsty suggested. "I'm sure that they will know what's going on."

Rachel, Kirsty and Mia flitted quickly to the gilded throne room.

Inside, several anxious-looking fairies surrounded the fairy royals. Rachel and Kirsty curtseyed.

"Hello, Your Majesties," Rachel said politely.

"We're very glad to see you, girls," said Queen Titania in her silvery voice. "These are the other fairies who work with Mia in the workshop."

Each fairy curtseyed to the girls, but they all looked very miserable.

"Why is the workshop closed, Your Majesties?" asked Mia.

"Everything the fairies try to make falls apart," said King Oberon sadly.

"Yesterday was a fairy wedding party," Queen Titania explained to Rachel and Kirsty. "We have one every year to thank the fairies in the Wedding Workshop for all their hard work. I will show you what happened."

She led them to the Seeing Pool in the palace gardens and waved her wand over the glassy surface. It swirled like a whirlpool and then settled, and a picture appeared.

Lots of fairies, goblins, elves, imps and pixies were dancing inside the palace ballroom.

A string quartet of frog musicians played wonderful music.

"Look, there's Jack Frost!" cried Rachel.

Tall, icy Jack Frost was standing alone in the corner of the ballroom with his arms folded and a sulky expression on his face. He beckoned to some of his goblin servants and led them into the dining hall. Inside, tall cakes towered over platters of cream puffs, sweet trifles, bouquets of ice-cream cones and colourful jellies. There were melt-in-the-mouth pastries, chocolate fountains, and even a meringue swan with sweets in the hollow of its back.

"I'll teach them not to ask me to dance!" snarled Jack Frost. "Tuck in!"

With a cheer of greedy delight, the goblins hurled themselves at the feast. The tall cakes splattered to the floor and jellies and ice creams whizzed through the air. Some of the goblins jumped into the chocolate fountain, and the meringue swan was trampled into a sticky mess.

"Jack Frost!" cried a voice.

The king and queen stood in the doorway.

"You were a welcome guest in our palace, but you have spoiled the feast for everyone!" said the queen.

"When I attend a party, I expect all the attention!" bellowed Jack Frost.

In the picture, Mia appeared behind the king and queen.

"This is a wedding party!" she cried.

"The fairies from the Wedding Workshop are the guests of honour, not you!"

"Be quiet, you silly fairy!" Jack snapped.

"You and your goblins need to learn that greediness and bad manners don't pay," said King Oberon sternly. "Go home. You are not welcome at the rest of the celebrations."

Enraged, Jack Frost pointed a thin, icy finger at Mia.

"*You'll* regret this!" he hissed.

The image faded.

"While Mia was on her way to visit Rachel and Kirsty earlier today, Jack Frost ambushed the Wedding Workshop, stole the wedding charms and sent his goblins to hide them in the human world," said Queen Titania, gravely.

Mia's eyes filled with tiny, sparkling tears.

"*All* of them?" she asked in a trembling voice.

The queen nodded and put her arm around the little fairy, whose wings were drooping miserably.

"What exactly *are* the wedding charms?" asked Kirsty.

"They are three magical items that recharge Mia's magic powers," the queen explained. "They also make weddings go smoothly. The Silver Sixpence ensures that the married couple will prosper all their lives."

"The Golden Bells are a good luck

charm," added the king. "And the Moonshine Veil brings happiness."

"But without the charms, Mia's powers will weaken and disappear," the queen finished.

"Oh no!" Rachel gasped, clasping Mia's hand.

"This could ruin every wedding in the human world!" Mia cried.

The Wishing Well

"Mia, do you think you can find the charms before it's too late?" asked the queen.

"I'll do everything I can," said Mia in a determined voice.

"We'll help!" the girls chimed in eagerly.

The queen smiled at them. "I was hoping you would say that!"

"How will we know where to start looking?" asked Rachel.

"I have a special connection to the charms," said Mia. "The closer I am to them, the stronger my magic feels. That should help us to find them."

"Oh, let's start looking straightaway!" said Kirsty. "There's no time to lose!"

Queen Titania smiled at the girls gratefully and waved her wand.

"Good luck!" she said.

"Thank you, goodbye!" called Rachel and Kirsty.

Mia and the girls disappeared in a glittering whirl of fairy dust.

A moment later, they found themselves back in the alley next to Kenbury High Street.

"Will you tell us more about each charm so we can work out a plan?" Rachel asked Mia eagerly.

"Well," Mia began, "the Silver Sixpence is the least powerful of the charms. It is traditionally used to help couples prosper, but in the wrong hands it could be used to steal money."

"And greedy goblin hands are definitely the wrong hands!" said Kirsty with a sigh.

Suddenly, Mia gave a cry of excitement. She rose above them, flitting left and right.

"I can sense that the Silver Sixpence

has been here!" she gasped. "If we hurry, we can follow the goblins!"

Quickly, Mia flew off and the girls followed her. Soon they were flitting over the purple heather of a large moor. Mia pointed at a small village just ahead.

"The Silver Sixpence is somewhere there," she declared. "I'm sure of it."

As they fluttered towards the village, Rachel gave a surprised cry.

"I came here on holiday once!" she said excitedly. "It's famous because it has the oldest *wishing well* in the country!"

Kirsty gasped, understanding her best friend at once. "In the human world, people throw *coins* into wishing wells," she explained to Mia.

"Perhaps the goblins have seen humans making wishes, and now they are trying to use the Silver Sixpence to wish for more money!" Rachel added eagerly.

Sure enough, they soon spotted a group of goblins standing around the wishing well, arguing loudly. The girls landed close by and hid behind a tree trunk.

"You idiot!" they heard one goblin snap. "Why did you throw it in there?"

"I wished for all the money in the world, but nothing happened!" wailed another, who had a large wart on his nose.

"The Silver Sixpence would never respond to a greedy wish like that!" whispered Mia indignantly.

"So now we have NO money and NO Silver Sixpence!" roared a third goblin, poking the warty one in the chest with his long finger. "Do you fancy explaining that to Jack Frost, pea-brain?"

"You have to get it back," the first goblin declared.

"Not me!" squealed the warty one. "I'm scared of the dark!"

"Tough luck," said another goblin. "You should have thought of that before!"

He grabbed the warty goblin's ankles and dangled him upside down over the well.

"Eeek! Let me go!"
shrieked the goblin.

But another goblin seized
the second one's ankles and
dangled him into the well.
The warty one dropped
down even lower.

"NO!" he wailed, his
voice echoing around the
curved walls.

One by one, each goblin
grabbed the ankles of the
goblin in front, making a
bony, green chain out of
their own bodies.

"You're squeezing my
ankles too hard!" yelled one.

"It makes me dizzy being upside
down!" another complained. "I feel sick!"

"Shut up and get on with it!" bellowed the goblin at the top of the well, who had to hold on to them all.

With groans and moans, they slowly lowered the warty goblin down to the bottom of the well.

"We have to find the Silver Sixpence before they do," Kirsty whispered in dismay. "But how?"

"I've got an idea!" Rachel said suddenly, her eyes gleaming. "Mia, can you use your magic to make some fake silver sixpences?"

"Yes," said Mia, "my magic powers are stronger because the Silver Sixpence is so close. But how will that help?"

"If we can confuse the goblins with the fake coins, we'll have more chance of getting our hands on the real Silver Sixpence!" Rachel explained.

"That's a great plan!" cried Mia in excitement. "And my fairy magic can make the coins disappear as soon as the goblins touch them! Come on!"

Mia and the girls flitted towards the dark well. Rachel's heart began to thump. Could they trick the goblins and avoid being caught?

"Fairies!" shrieked one goblin, as Mia and the girls entered the well. "Don't let them find the coin!"

The goblin chain was still nowhere near the water at the well's bottom. But the second goblin let go of the warty one's ankles, and he fell the rest of the way down, howling loudly. He landed in the water with a loud splash.

"Quick, find it!" shouted the other goblins, who were still dangling down the side of the well.

Mia and the girls hovered just above the water, and then Mia waved her wand and created a fake sixpence.

"Got it!" she called loudly, holding it up to show the goblins...

Coin Confusion

Mia fluttered away from the goblin, clutching the fake coin. The other goblins yelled instructions as loud as they could.

"After her!"

"Stop her!"

"Go right!"

"Faster!"

Confused by all the shouting, the goblin chased Mia round and round the well, while Kirsty and Rachel dived

underwater. None of the goblins were
watching them. Their plan was working!

The bottom of the well was
covered in coins, but one
had a beautiful silvery
glow. The girls felt
sure that it was the
real Silver Sixpence
and they carefully
picked it up.

The goblin finally caught up with Mia
and snatched the fake sixpence out of
her hand. But as soon as his clammy
fingers touched the coin, it disappeared!
The watching goblins gave howls of
rage. Just then, Rachel and Kirsty rose
out of the water and nodded at Mia. She
flicked her wand and a fake coin
appeared in Rachel's hands, while Kirsty

hid the real Silver Sixpence behind
her back.

"*She's* got it!" yelled one of the goblins,
pointing at Rachel.

All the goblins' eyes turned towards
Rachel, and they didn't pay any
attention to Kirsty as she flew swiftly out
of the well, carrying the real Silver
Sixpence. Rachel started to pretend that
the coin was too heavy for her.

"Help!" she called to Mia.
"I'm not strong enough!"

"I'm coming!" Mia cried.

"Get her!" the goblins yelled.

The warty goblin flung himself
towards Rachel, but just in time she lifted
herself out of his reach! She flapped
upwards, pretending to pant with
the effort.

"NO!" screamed the watching goblins. "She's getting away!"

"Come down and help me, then!" snapped the warty goblin, jumping up and down and trying to catch Rachel.

The goblin at the top of the well swung the goblin chain outwards, and five dangling goblins launched themselves at Rachel in a jumble of arms and legs. Then he jumped down too, aiming for Rachel and her coin!

Rachel flung herself against the side of the well and dropped the fake coin. All the goblins splash-landed in a green, tangled heap at the bottom of the well.

"Find that coin!" spluttered the muffled voice of the warty goblin from the bottom of the pile.

Giggling, Mia joined Rachel and they fluttered upwards out of the well.

"Those pesky fairies are getting away!" shrieked another goblin.

"Never mind them!" yelled a third, scrabbling around in the water. "Find the Silver Sixpence!"

Kirsty was waiting at the top of the well, holding the real Silver Sixpence and grinning.

"It worked like a charm!" Rachel laughed.

"Thank you so much for helping me," said Mia. "I feel stronger already!"

With a touch of her wand, she returned the coin to its Fairyland size. Then she put

it into a little silk pouch that she tucked
into a pocket in her dress.
The shouts of the goblins
echoed around the well.

"Let's go!" Mia advised.
"It won't be long before
they realise they've been
tricked!"

Sure enough, as they flew
away, they heard a chorus of
enraged shrieks.

"I think they just found the last fake
coin — and it vanished!" giggled Kirsty.

Back in Kenbury, near Aunt Isabel's
house, Mia returned the girls to their
normal size.

"I'm going to take the Silver Sixpence
back to its home in the Wedding
Workshop!" she said happily. "Thank

60

you so much, girls. I'm sure I'll see you again very soon! We still have a difficult task ahead – we need to find the other two charms!"

Rachel and Kirsty nodded and waved goodbye.

"I'm so glad that we found the Silver Sixpence!" Rachel grinned.

"Me too," Kirsty replied. "I just hope that we can find the other charms before Saturday!"

"Don't worry, we won't let Jack Frost spoil Esther's wedding," said Rachel in a determined voice. "We've got Mia to help us, and we've got each other. I just know we'll succeed!"

The Golden Bells

Contents

A Charming Challenge

"I can't believe how many things there are to think about for just one wedding," Kirsty said, peering into a display case in the jewellery shop. "I'm not surprised that Mia needs help in the Wedding Workshop!"

That morning, Esther and her mum had taken the girls to Bickwood, the nearby town. Esther needed some jewellery to wear when she left for her honeymoon.

"These necklaces are so pretty," said Rachel.

"They look as delicate as if they had been made by fairies!" Kirsty replied.

"Perhaps Esther could use the necklace she buys today as the 'something new'?" suggested Rachel.

"But it's for her honeymoon, not for the wedding," Kirsty sighed. Then her eyes brightened. "Of course! Esther's wedding dress has been made especially for her! That could be the 'something new'!"

"Perfect!" Rachel exclaimed. "Now we just have to find 'something borrowed' and 'something blue'!"

They stopped beside a table where several pretty jewellery boxes and pouches were displayed.

"I bet India the Moonstone Fairy would love this shop," Kirsty said quietly to Rachel, remembering the adventures they had shared with the Jewel Fairies. "And—oh!"

A purple, velvet jewellery pouch had fallen off the table and landed on the floor in front of them. Rachel bent down and picked it up.

"Kirsty, look!" she exclaimed. Two initials were embroidered in gold on the pouch – R and K.

Kirsty's eyes shone. "Do you think it might be magic?"

Rachel nodded excitedly and opened the pouch. Mia flew out in a flurry of fairy dust!

"Hello, girls!" she whispered, whizzing over to hide on Kirsty's shoulder.

The girls quickly moved to a quiet part of the shop where no one could overhear them.

"Mia!" whispered Kirsty in delight. "How are you?"

"Not great," Mia admitted. "Things are going wrong for weddings all over the world!"

"At least the poor bridesmaids have you to help them," said Rachel.

"Yes, and I'm feeling stronger

now that the Silver Sixpence is safe, although my magic is still not as powerful as usual," said Mia. "But girls, I think that the goblins have taken the Golden Bells to a Caribbean island!"

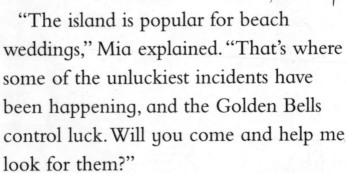

"How can you be sure?" asked Rachel.

"The island is popular for beach weddings," Mia explained. "That's where some of the unluckiest incidents have been happening, and the Golden Bells control luck. Will you come and help me look for them?"

"Of course!" replied Rachel eagerly.

Kirsty hurried over to her cousin and aunt.

"Aunt Isabel, can we go off by ourselves for a while?" she asked. "We want to look for something that will make Esther's wedding extra special."

"Yes, all right dear," smiled Aunt Isabel. "But don't be long."

Kirsty and Rachel hurried outside and dashed up an alleyway. Mia waved her wand and sprinkled fairy dust over them. Immediately the girls shrank to fairy size and fluttered their wings in delight. However many wonderful adventures they shared with their fairy friends, it was always thrilling to be able to fly!

"We must get to the island as quickly as we can," said Mia.

She flicked her wand again, and a white, puffy cloud drifted towards them. By the time it reached them, it had transformed into a gleaming white carriage, pulled by four white cloud horses!

Mia and the girls climbed in, and the
horses whisked them into the blue sky.
Rachel and Kirsty snuggled back into
their seats, feeling the cloud shape itself
around them, as Mia told them the story
of the Golden Bells.

"Many years ago, King Oberon rescued a leprechaun from some goblins who were playing tricks on him," Mia said.

"He was lost and tired, so the king gave him good food and a warm bed. Before the leprechaun left, he gave the king two of the lucky gold bells from his cap to thank him."

"What a lovely present!" said Kirsty, her eyes shining.

"The king wanted to bless everyone with the leprechaun's gift," Mia went on. "So he gave the bells to me, to bring luck to all weddings."

"Kirsty, we just have to find the Golden Bells!" said Rachel. "We can't let Jack Frost and his goblins use all that luck for their own benefit!"

They felt the carriage sinking lower in the sky. After a gentle bump, the door opened and they tumbled out on to the white sand of a Caribbean beach. With a wave of Mia's wand the cloud horses whinnied and pulled the carriage into the air again. As they went, they seemed to lose their shape, and soon they were just ordinary clouds again.

Mia was looking pale. "I'm feeling a bit weak," she said. "That used up more magic than I thought."

"Don't worry," said Kirsty, squeezing her hand. "We'll soon find the Golden Bells and recharge your magic."

The girls brushed the fine sand off their clothes and gazed around in delight. Tall palm trees waved in a warm breeze, and the sun glittered on the foaming waves.

"This is the most amazing beach I've ever seen!" Kirsty smiled.

"Perhaps the luck of the Golden Bells will help us find them straightaway," said Rachel. "Then we'll have time to explore!"

But Mia's wings drooped sadly. "The
luck only works for whoever last touched
the Golden Bells," she said. "And of
course, that was the goblins."

Kirsty and Rachel exchanged
determined looks.

"Don't worry, Mia," said Rachel,
putting her arm around the little fairy's
shoulders. "We will get the Golden Bells
back from those
naughty goblins!"

"Perhaps
luck is on
our side
after all!"
said Kirsty,
pointing
further down
the beach.

A group of goblins were playing beach volleyball, capering around in brightly patterned shorts. One was wearing flippers on his feet and another had swimming goggles around his head. Suntan lotion was smeared all over their noses and cheeks.

Suddenly the
goblin in flippers
tripped over his
feet and missed
the ball.

"Ten points to
us!" shouted a
goblin in a flowery swimming cap.

"No it isn't!" snapped the goblin
wearing flippers.

Looking furious, the first goblin pushed

him over.
"I'll get
you for
that!" the
one in
flippers
shrieked
with rage.

He flung himself at the other and they rolled around on the sand, yelling fiercely. The other goblins piled on top of them and Rachel shook her head in amazement.

"They must really enjoy squabbling, because they even do it on holiday!" she exclaimed.

Then she gave a gasp and pointed. On a long ribbon, dangling from a nearby palm tree, were the Golden Bells!

Hide and Seek

The girls and Mia fluttered towards
the palm tree, staying out of sight.
Lizards and hermit crabs scurried out
of their way.

"Over here!" whispered Rachel,
ducking behind a large, fallen coconut
under the tree.

87

Kirsty and Mia joined her and glanced over at the goblins. The argument was over and they had started to play volleyball again. The girls were almost underneath the Golden Bells.

"I could just fly up and get them!" said Mia eagerly.

"Wait – what if the goblins see you?" cried Kirsty.

But Mia rose off the ground, and Kirsty and Rachel held their breath. Mia's fingers had almost reached the Golden Bells when... THUMP! A volleyball banged against the tree, flinging the Golden Bells into the air.

With a chiming sound they landed in the
arms of a goblin whose shorts were
patterned with blue daisies. Rachel and
Kirsty flew up to join Mia, and the
goblin saw them.

"Fairies!" he shouted.

"They can't do anything!" sneered
another, who was wearing bright orange
arm bands. "Luck is on our side!"

"Oh no, they know about the luck!"
Rachel thought, groaning inwardly.

"Let's go and play somewhere else,"
said the blue-daisy goblin.

"Wait!" cried Rachel desperately.
"Can't you see that you're ruining
wedding days everywhere?"

"Can't *you* see that *we* don't care?"
jeered the goblin.

"I think it's better if they don't see

anything at all!" said another in a mocking, singsong voice.

He picked up a handful of sand and threw it at the girls and Mia!

"Close your eyes!" Mia cried.

Rachel and Kirsty squeezed their eyes shut as the sand rained down on them. They could hear sniggering and running footsteps. But when they opened their eyes again, the goblins were nowhere to be seen.

"They must have run like the wind!" Kirsty said crossly.

"It's the luck of the Golden Bells working against us," said Mia sadly. "But we have to find them…and quickly!"

Mia and the girls fluttered over trees, peered into caves and flew around rocks and bushes, keeping their eyes peeled for a glint of goblin green or a flash of gold. But the longer they looked, the paler Mia became.

"I feel really tired," she said with a sigh. "It took a lot of magical energy to bring us here, and we've been searching for ages.

I'll have to go back to Fairyland and use the Silver Sixpence to recharge my magic."

"Wait!" said Rachel, holding up her hand. "Can you hear something?"

They all paused and listened. Kirsty nodded eagerly.

"It sounds like…goblins!" she said.

Kirsty, Rachel and Mia flew around a cluster of tall palm trees.

"Look!" Rachel gasped in excitement.

They saw a large pool at the base of a frothing waterfall. And swinging across the pool on ropes, yelling, squealing and screeching, was a gaggle of goblins!

Treetop Trouble

"Oh, those naughty goblins!" Mia exclaimed. "They are making a terrible nuisance of themselves."

"Whoopee!" yelled two goblins, dive-bombing into the pool.

Fish swam out of the way and flamingos scattered in pink confusion as the goblins' screeches echoed around the clearing.

95

"Geronimo!" hollered another.

He somersaulted under the waterfall, splashing water into the undergrowth. A flock of parrots rose into the air, squawking crossly.

There seemed to be goblins everywhere. But where were the Golden Bells?

"Let's fly around the pool and see if Mia can sense which direction they were taken in," said Kirsty.

They started to flutter around the pool,
holding Mia's hands to help her.

Suddenly, she gave a gasp.

"I felt a prickle of magic all
down my back!" she
exclaimed.

"The Golden Bells
must be in that
direction!" said
Rachel.

The three
friends fluttered
away from the
pool, and soon
Mia let go of the
girls' hands.

"I'm feeling stronger
already," she said. "We're
getting closer!"

After flying for a few more minutes,
they reached a clearing and Kirsty gave
a cry. There was a glint of gold amid
the green! The Golden Bells were
hanging from a high branch on their
ribbon, but...

"Oh no!" said Rachel in a whisper.

Two goblin guards were there too,
clutching on tightly to the
branch. They were so
pale green that they
were almost white.

"You've got
more room than
me!" whimpered
the first goblin,
who had
swimming goggles
around his head.

98

"I've got no room at all!" trembled the other, who was still wearing his flowery swimming cap.

"It was your silly idea to draw straws to decide who would guard the Golden Bells," the goggled goblin snivelled.

"But why did you have to hide them in the tallest tree?" gulped the other, looking down and then covering his eyes.

"Hey, stop pushing me!" the first goblin complained.

"You're the one pushing me!" whined the second goblin, giving him a shove.

They lost their grip on the branch
and tumbled backwards out of the tree!

The goblin with the flowery cap
hooked his toe over a
branch below. He
grabbed the other
by his swimming
trunks and they
dangled upside
down.

"That was
lucky!" Rachel
gasped.

Mia nodded. "It
was the luck of
the Golden Bells."

"You've made my goggles fall off!"
wailed the first goblin, clambering back
up to the branch.

"You pushed us off the branch in the first place!" grumbled the goblin in the swimming cap.

"Didn't!

"Did!"

They started to climb back up the tree, bickering as they went.

"Now's our chance!" Kirsty said.

"I'll fly to the end of the branch and unhook the Golden Bells!" said Mia.

But Rachel shook her head.

"We can't," she said firmly. "If we fly away with the Golden Bells, the goblins' luck will change. They're bound to fall out of the tree and hurt themselves!"

"You're right," said Mia, her shoulders sagging.

"Mia, can you magic the goblins to the ground safely?" asked Kirsty.

"Yes," said Mia. "But only if I've touched the Golden Bells and got their luck on my side."

"Then that's what you'll have to do," Kirsty declared. "Touch the Golden Bells and magic the goblins safely to the ground before they can grab us!"

"You'll have to be quick," added Rachel in alarm. "They've almost reached the branch!"

Something Blue

As the goblins lunged for the branch,
Mia and the girls tried to tug the ribbon
loose. Shrieking with rage, the goblins
shoved the girls away.

"Help!" cried Kirsty. "I'm falling!"

The girls and the goblins lost their
balance and went tumbling towards the
ground, a tangled mass of arms, legs
and wings!

"Fairies, use your magic!" screamed the goblins.

"My wand arm is trapped!" Mia cried.

THUMP! They landed in a jumbled heap on a soft pile of moss and leaves. There was a chiming tinkle as the Golden Bells landed nearby.

"Hang on. . ." said Rachel, untangling her wings from the goblins' legs.

"Wait a minute. . ." said one of the goblins.

"Who was the last to touch the Golden Bells?" they cried together.

They had no idea whose side the luck was on!

The goblins and the girls made a dash for the Golden Bells at exactly the same moment. But one of the goblins tripped on a root and the other stubbed his toe on a rock. Mia reached the Golden Bells first, and the girls realised it must have been Mia who had touched them last!

The goblins gave cries of rage as they hopped around the clearing, clutching their sore toes.

"I'm not explaining this to Jack Frost!" wailed the first one.

"Nor me!" the other declared.

They disappeared into the forest, their voices fading away. Rachel and Kirsty sighed with relief.

Just then, something
twirled down to them
from the sky and
landed next to
Kirsty, who picked
it up.

"Look!" she
said. "It's a
feather!"

It was a
brilliant blue
colour that
shimmered
and gleamed
in the light.

"Oh, Rachel!" Kirsty exclaimed
suddenly. "This can be our 'something
blue' for Esther!"

"You're right!" Rachel agreed.

"Thank you both so much for helping me to find the Golden Bells!" Mia said with a smile.

With a twirl of her wand, she restored the Golden Bells to their Fairyland size and put them into a silk pouch which she tucked into her dress.

She gave another wave of her wand, and
Rachel and Kirsty closed their eyes as a
whirl of sparkling confetti surrounded
them. When they opened their eyes
again, they were standing in a quiet road
next to the jewellery shop in Bickwood.

"Thank you again, girls," said Mia. "I'm going to hurry back to Fairyland and return the Golden Bells. But I'll see you very soon – after all, we still need to find the Moonlight Veil!"

She disappeared in a flurry of sparkles and the girls walked back into the shop.

"Hi girls!" Esther called. "Come and tell me which earrings to choose. I just can't decide!"

Rachel and Kirsty hurried over and looked at all the jewellery in the case.

There were diamond studs, dangling
pendants and pretty flower shapes. But
Rachel and Kirsty knew exactly which
ones to pick. They both pointed at a
pair of earrings in the shape of tiny,
golden bells!

The Moonshine
Veil

Contents

Shooting
Star

"Just one more night to go!" said Kirsty,
as she brushed her hair. "Isn't it exciting?"

Rachel nodded eagerly, and then sighed.
"I won't be able to enjoy it properly if
we haven't found the Moonshine Veil,"
she said, climbing into bed. "I'll be too
worried about the mischief Jack Frost
and his goblins will make."

"That's true," agreed Kirsty, looking thoughtful.

The door opened and Mrs Tate popped her head round.

"Are you ready for bed, girls?" she asked.

"Yes, Mum," said Kirsty. "Is everything OK downstairs?"

"I think so!" laughed Mrs Tate. "I've been practising hairstyles on your Aunt Isabel while she double-checked the seating plans. Esther is finishing the orders of service with some of her friends."

"It sounds as if all of Kenbury is here this evening!" said Rachel with a grin.

The house had been packed with friends, family and neighbours all day, and the sound of laughter still floated up the stairs.

"We're all helping to make the final checks," said Mrs Tate with a smile.

"What are you checking, Mum?" Kirsty asked.

"Oh, all the hundreds of tiny details that go into making the perfect wedding," said Mrs Tate with a wink. "Goodnight, girls. I'll see you bright and early in the morning!"

She turned off the main light and closed the door behind her.

"I keep thinking about all the things that could go *wrong* tomorrow," Kirsty said.

"Me too," Rachel added nervously, sitting up in bed. "Unless the Moonshine Veil is found, anything could happen at the wedding, and it's bound to be something to do with us bridesmaids."

"And we still haven't thought of the 'something borrowed'," Kirsty said, walking over to the window and opening it.

"But let's try not to worry too much. I'm sure we can help Esther to have the perfect day!"

She leaned out and breathed in the
fresh country air. In the distance,
she could see the lights of Bickwood
twinkling. Rachel joined her and
together they looked up at the moonlit,
star-filled sky.

"You can always see ten times as
many stars in the country," said Kirsty.

"I know," Rachel agreed. "Oh Kirsty –
look!"

She pointed up to where a shooting
star was burning across the sky.

"Quickly, make a wish!" Kirsty exclaimed.

They closed their eyes and made their wishes. When they opened their eyes again, Kirsty frowned.

"That's funny," she said. "The shooting star isn't fading. It seems to be getting bigger."

Sure enough, the burning star was getting brighter…and brighter…and brighter!

"It's coming straight at us!" Rachel cried.

They jumped aside and the star shot between them onto the carpet, fizzing and crackling. When it faded, Mia was standing in front of them, with a smile as bright as the star itself!

A Fake Feast

"Hello again, girls!" called Mia.

"Hello Mia!" cried Rachel and Kirsty in delight.

"Have you found the Moonshine Veil?" asked Kirsty hopefully.

"Not yet," Mia replied. "But this is the best time to search for it. In the dark it glows just like the moon, and there's a lunar eclipse tonight!"

Rachel frowned. "What's that?"

"The Earth is going to pass between the moon and the sun," said Mia, creating a magical picture with her wand to show what this looked like.

"It will block the light from the sun, and Earth's shadow will cover the moon. That means that the only moonlight will be coming from the Moonshine Veil."

"So it should be easy to spot!" Rachel exclaimed.

"But we still don't know where the Moonshine Veil is," added Kirsty.

Suddenly, Rachel's eyes lit up.

"I've got an idea," she said. "We all know that the greedy goblins can't resist food. Mia, do you think you could magic up a delicious feast…?"

"Yes," said Mia. "But how will a feast help?"

"If the goblins are nearby, I'm sure that they will try to steal the food!" Rachel explained.

"You're right!" Kirsty cried.

"It's a bit risky to lead the goblins to us deliberately," Mia warned them.

Rachel and Kirsty looked at each
other. It was a little bit scary to think
of facing lots of goblins, but if they didn't
find the Moonshine Veil tonight, Esther's
wedding might be ruined.

"We have to risk it!" Rachel said
determinedly.

Mia swished her wand and glittering
fairy dust whirled around the girls.

They felt themselves shrinking to fairy size, and they fluttered their gossamer wings excitedly. Then they flew out of the window, down the lane and out of the village to a dark, empty field and landed next to a clump of daisies.

Mia flicked her wand and a marvellous feast appeared. Delicious-looking food was laid out on a large blanket. There were piles of cucumber sandwiches, hot jacket potatoes with melting butter and cheese, jugs of lemonade, chocolate cupcakes and bowls filled with strawberries and cream.

"Now all we can do is wait," said Mia. Almost as soon as they had hidden themselves behind the daisies, they heard jabbering voices. A group of goblins crept into the field. All were carrying rucksacks, and the girls could see a large net poking out of one of them. Rachel nudged Kirsty and pointed. One of the rucksacks was glowing silvery-blue.

"The Moonshine Veil!" Kirsty
exclaimed.

As the goblins reached for the food,
it disappeared. Mia, Rachel and Kirsty
fluttered out from their hiding place and
faced the goblins.

"Give back the Moonshine Veil!" Mia
demanded. "It doesn't belong to you!"

"You tricksy fairies!" shrieked the
tallest goblin.

"Please, give back the veil," Kirsty said.
"Mia will reward you with as many
cakes as you can eat."

"Mmm, cakes," said a plump goblin.
"I like the sound of that."

"It's a trick!" said the
tall goblin.
"The cakes
will just
vanish like
the feast!"

"But I'm
really
hungry!"
wailed the
first. "Let's
give them
the silly
veil!"

Mia and Kirsty were distracted by the
squabbling goblins, but Rachel suddenly
turned pale.

"Kirsty," she said, "how many goblins did you see come into the field?"

"Er…seven," Kirsty replied. "Why?"

"Because now there are only five of them," cried Rachel.

They whirled around – just as the two remaining goblins threw the net over them from behind!

Eclipse of the Moon

The other goblins stopped fighting and tied the net shut with a rope.

"Oh no!" whispered Mia. "I've dropped my wand!"

"Teehee!" cackled the tall goblin. "We've tricked the tricksy fairies!"

They put their
thumbs on
their noses
and
waggled
their
fingers at
Mia and the
girls, who were
squashed together
in the tied-up net. Then they ran off in
the direction of Bickwood.

"Ouch!" exclaimed Rachel. "I think
you've got your elbow in my ear,
Kirsty."

"Sorry," panted Kirsty, moving it.

"Ooh, now it's in my ear!" said Mia.

"Sorry!" cried Kirsty again. "Oh dear,
what are we going to do?"

"Mia, can you magic us out of here?" asked Rachel.

"Not without my wand," Mia sighed.

"We've got to get out of here fast or the goblins will get away!" Rachel exclaimed.

"Girls!" cried Mia suddenly. "Listen!"

They heard a loud snuffling noise. A brown fieldmouse was scurrying towards them.

"Excuse me," called Mia. "Please can you help us? We're stuck!"

The little mouse sat up on its back legs and sniffed the air. Its whiskers twitched. Then it hurried over and nibbled at the net. Soon it had made a hole large enough for the friends to clamber through. As Mia picked up her wand, she kissed the tip of the fieldmouse's nose. "Thank you so much!" she whispered. Mia waved her wand and a pile of nuts and berries appeared in front of the mouse.

Then the three friends fluttered their
crumpled wings and rose into the air.
As they flew towards Bickwood, the
night seemed to grow darker.

"The eclipse of the moon is almost complete!" Rachel cried.

As the Earth's shadow finally covered the moon, one street remained bathed in moonlight.

"*That's* where the Moonshine Veil is!" cried Mia in triumph.

"And the goblins!" Rachel reminded her.

The light was coming from a wedding
shop. The girls peered through the
window and gasped.

The shop was crawling with goblins,
swathed in veils, wedding dresses, hats
and high heels. One of them was
walking with his arms held out,
balancing wobbling tiaras on his head.

Another was wearing a gold brocade
pageboy outfit. He was pinching the
arms of a goblin in a pink frilly
bridesmaid dress.

"Get off!" yelled
the goblin in
the dress.

He tried to
kick out, but
his foot got
caught in a frill
and he tripped
himself over.

Rachel, Kirsty and Mia slipped into the
shop through the letterbox and fluttered
behind a large hat. Somewhere among
those frothy dresses, pink frills and
beribboned goblins was the precious
Moonshine Veil...But where?

A Visit from Jack Frost...?

"I bet Jack Frost would be furious if he could see them messing around!" Mia said.

"You've just given me an idea!" Kirsty exclaimed. "Mia, could you make my voice sound like Jack Frost's?"

Mia nodded thoughtfully, then waved her wand towards Kirsty.

"Has it worked?" Kirsty asked in a growly whisper.

"You sound exactly like him!" Rachel gasped.

"You'd better be quick," Mia said. "The magic won't last long."

Kirsty took a deep breath.

"What are you doing, you idiots?" she bellowed.

The goblins froze in terror.

"You should be hiding the Moonshine Veil, not enjoying yourselves!" Kirsty roared.

The goblins stared wildly around.

"W-we w-were j-just about to h-hide it, m-master!" stammered the goblin in the wedding dress.

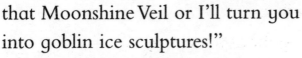

"You're useless!" Kirsty shouted. "Give me that Moonshine Veil or I'll turn you into goblin ice sculptures!"

Trembling, the goblin pulled a shimmering square of material from the bodice of the wedding dress. Mia darted forward excitedly, but Rachel stopped her.

"Not yet!" she whispered.

"Put it on the floor!" ordered Kirsty. "Then turn around!"

The goblins obeyed, and the girls flew out from their hiding place.

"Now shut your eyes!" Kirsty shouted.

But her voice cracked – the enchantment was wearing off! The goblins turned around, saw the girls, and immediately rushed forward. Hands pulled at the precious Moonshine Veil from all sides.

"It's going to tear!' Mia exclaimed. "We have to let go! We can't let it get ripped!"

In despair, Mia and the girls let go. But the goblins weren't expecting that! They all tumbled backwards, letting go of the Moonshine Veil, which flew into the air.

"Quickly, Mia!" Kirsty called out.

As Mia darted up and caught it, the Moonshine Veil shrank back down to fairy size.

The girls looked down at the goblins and giggled. The goblins had fallen backwards and crashed into racks of wedding dresses. All that could be seen were seven pairs of green legs waving in the air, surrounded by dresses, ribbons and veils.

"Get me out of here!" yelled a muffled voice from a frothy mass of lace.

Mia and the girls flew quickly out of
the letterbox and landed gently on the
pavement outside the shop.

"Thank you,
girls!" Mia said.
"I'll make
sure that the
shop is
tidied up
before
morning.
But first,
I must
return the
Moonshine Veil!"

"I've never seen
anything made of
moonlight before,"
said Rachel.

She and Kirsty gently touched the exquisite veil. It was so fine that they could hardly feel it under their fingers, and it lit up their faces with moonlight. It made them feel safe and warm just to look at it.

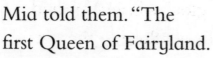

"It belonged to a very happy bride," Mia told them. "The first Queen of Fairyland. It's made from moonlight, and happiness is woven inside its threads."

She folded the veil into the tiniest square Rachel and Kirsty could imagine. It was now so small that the girls could

only see its blue–silver glow. Mia tucked
it into the silk pouch in a pocket in
her dress.

"Will you come with me to return it?"
she asked.

The girls nodded eagerly and Mia
looked up. The eclipse was ending, and
a single moonbeam was making a pool
of light on the pavement.

"Let's go!" she said.

Holding hands, Mia, Rachel and Kirsty
stepped into the pool of moonlight. At
once, the silvery glow whirled around
them, lifting them gently into the air.
They all closed their eyes and when they
opened them again, they were floating
over Fairyland!

Wedding Bells

They drifted towards the Fairyland Palace with its four pink turrets. Below they could see the king and queen, and all the fairies from the Wedding Workshop. Mia and the girls landed beside them, and Mia eagerly produced the Moonshine Veil. Everyone cheered happily.

"Well done, all of you!" cried Queen
Titania.

They hurried to the Wedding
Workshop, where an archway led
into a tiny, oval room with
three alcoves in the
wall. In the left-
hand alcove,
the Silver
Sixpence
was sitting
on a
cushion
of turquoise
satin. In the
right-hand alcove,
the Golden Bells
were lying on a
cushion of red silk.

"This is where the Moonshine Veil belongs," said Mia.

The centre alcove contained a small cushion of purple velvet. Mia laid the Moonshine Veil down, and the whole room glowed.

"Everything is in its place again," said Mia, beaming at the girls. "I have a present for you both to thank you for all your help."

She flicked her wand and a delicate chain appeared around each girl's ankle.

"Thank you!" gasped Rachel, whose anklet had a silver sixpence charm.

"Oh, it's beautiful!" whispered Kirsty, admiring the two tinkling gold bells on her anklet.

"I couldn't have done it without you,"
Mia said, hugging them.

"Now it is time for you to get ready to
be bridesmaids," said the queen. "Good
luck – and thank you!"

The queen waved her wand and
Rachel and Kirsty disappeared in a
sparkle of magic. All at once, they were
back in their bedroom and human-
sized again. Sunlight was
pouring in through
the open window.

"It's the wedding morning!" said Kirsty
excitedly.

Suddenly the
door burst
open and
Esther
rushed in.

"Girls, did
you manage
to find the
'somethings'?"
she asked anxiously.

Rachel and Kirsty smiled at each
other. They knew exactly what to
say and do. Kirsty held out her
grandmother's sparkling brooch.

"Something old," she said.

"Your wedding dress is something new,"
Rachel added.

"Something borrowed," Kirsty said, unfastening her golden anklet.

"And something blue," declared Rachel, producing the bird feather from the Caribbean.

"What an amazing colour!" said Esther. "It can go into my bouquet."

Rachel unhooked the silver sixpence charm from her anklet and held it out.

"And a sixpence in her shoe!" the girls chanted together.

Kirsty and Rachel had showers and then put on their lovely dresses. Mrs Tate decorated their hair with tiny white roses. Then Kirsty and Rachel went to help Esther. She looked like a princess in her ivory dress. The girls arranged the filmy veil over her long black curls.

"Oh girls, I'm so nervous!" Esther exclaimed.

"Don't be," said Kirsty with a happy laugh. "I just know that this is going to be an absolutely magical wedding!"

As the bride and groom stepped out of the church after the ceremony, confetti fluttered around their heads. Behind them, Kirsty and Rachel were smiling happily.

"Hasn't it been a wonderful morning?" Kirsty said. "I think my favourite bit was the horse-drawn carriage that brought us to the church!"

"Mine was following Esther down the aisle to the beautiful music," Rachel replied, her eyes sparkling.

Esther turned around and smiled at them.

"You've been the perfect bridesmaids, girls," she said. "Thank you!"

"Everyone say 'Cheese'!" called the photographer.

Kirsty and Rachel put their arms around each other's waist and exchanged a secret smile. They had a much better word.

"MAGIC!"

RAINBOW magic®

The Green Fairies

Now it's time for Rachel and Kirsty
to help the Green Fairies! The first
fairy they meet is

Nicole the Beach Fairy

Time for Action!

"Isn't it wonderful to be back on Rainspell Island again, Rachel?" Kirsty Tate said happily, gazing out over the shimmering, blue-green sea. "It hasn't changed a bit!"

Rachel Walker, Kirsty's best friend, nodded. "Rainspell is still as beautiful as ever, isn't it?" she replied, as the two girls followed the rocky path down to the beach. "This is one of the most special places in the whole world!"

The Tates and the Walkers were spending the half-term holiday on Rainspell Island. Although it was autumn, the sky was a clear blue and the sun was shining brightly, so it felt more like summer. Kirsty and Rachel couldn't wait to get to the beach and dip their toes in the sea.

"You're right, Rachel," Kirsty agreed, her eyes twinkling. "After all, this is where we first became friends!"

"And we found lots of other wonderful friends here too, didn't we?" Rachel laughed.

Kirsty and Rachel shared an amazing secret. During their first holiday on Rainspell Island, they'd met the Rainbow Fairies after Jack Frost's wicked spell had cast them out of Fairyland. Since then the girls had got to know many of the other fairies, and the tiny, magical friends often asked for Rachel and Kirsty's help whenever Jack Frost and his naughty goblin servants were causing problems.

"This is gorgeous!" Kirsty said, as they reached the beach at last.

The flat, golden sand seemed to stretch for miles into the distance. Seagulls soared in the sky above, and Kirsty could smell the fresh, salty sea air. "Shall we explore the rock pools, Rachel?" she suggested.

But Rachel didn't reply. She was looking along the beach, her face clouded with dismay.

"Haven't you noticed the litter, Kirsty?" she asked, pointing ahead of them.

Kirsty stared at the golden sand more closely. To her horror, down near the sea's edge, she could see a couple of plastic bags blowing around in the light breeze. There were also some drinks cans and empty water bottles floating in the sea...

Win Rainbow Magic Goodies!

There are lots of Rainbow Magic fairies, and we want to know which one is your favourite! Send us a picture of her and tell us in thirty words why she is your favourite and why you like Rainbow Magic books. Each month we will put the entries into a draw and select one winner to receive a Rainbow Magic Sparkly T-shirt and Goody Bag!

Send your entry on a postcard to Rainbow Magic Competition, Orchard Books, 338 Euston Road, London NW1 3BH.
Australian readers should email: childrens.books@hachette.com.au
New Zealand readers should write to Rainbow Magic Competition, 4 Whetu Place, Mairangi Bay, Auckland NZ.
Don't forget to include your name and address.
Only one entry per child.

Good luck!

Look out for the Green Fairies!

NICOLE
THE BEACH FAIRY
978-1-40830-474-7

ISABELLA
THE AIR FAIRY
978-1-40830-475-4

EDIE
THE GARDEN FAIRY
978-1-40830-476-1

CORAL
THE REEF FAIRY
978-1-40830-477-8

LILY
THE RAINFOREST FAIRY
978-1-40830-478-5

MILLY
THE RIVER FAIRY
978-1-40830-480-8

CARRIE
THE SNOW CAP FAIRY
978-1-40830-479-2

Out now!